To my loving parents, Ted and Fran Walter. They moved our family to Manhattan when I was three, where I grew up a natural Wildcat fan. Go Cats!

- Dan Walter

For Sue, Ana Milagros, and Angel Miguel

~ Miguel De Angel

www.mascotbooks.com

For more information, please contact:
Mascot Books
560 Herndon Parkway #120
Herndon, VA 20170
info@mascotbooks.com

3rd Printing 2013

CPSIA Code: PRT0113C
ISBN-10: 1-932888-52-7
ISBN-13: 978-1-932888-52-2

Printed in the United States

Hello, Willie!

Dan Walter

**Illustrated by Miguel De Angel
with T. Scholes, J. Hilton & E. Saenz**

It was a beautiful fall day in
Manhattan, Kansas.

Willie the Wildcat was on his way to watch a Kansas State football game.

As Willie walked through Aggieville,
some Wildcat fans said, "Hello, Willie!"

Willie took time to pose
for several pictures.

Willie could hear the bells
ringing at Anderson Hall.

He took a few minutes to
enjoy the beautiful melody.

Willie then walked by the K-State Student Union where he met many students on their way to the game.

After he took time to sign autographs,
the students said, "Thanks, Willie!"

Willie walked by the University
Gardens where he smelled
the beautiful flowers.

Suddenly, a fire truck filled with cheerleaders pulled up. They yelled, "Hop on, Willie, or you'll be late to the game!"

Thanks to his friends, Willie the Wildcat
arrived at Bill Snyder Family Stadium
in plenty of time for the game.

He waved at the many
fans entering the stadium.
The fans yelled, "Hello, Willie!"

Soon, the game began.
The Wildcat defense stopped
the visiting team for a loss.

Willie led the crowd in a
K-S-U Wildcats cheer!

At halftime, the K-State
Marching Band put on a great show.

Willie especially enjoyed
"The Wabash Cannonball" song!

Willie joined the crowd in cheering
when the offense made another
"Wildcat first down!"

When K-State scored another touchdown, Willie did push-ups for every point! It was a lot of push-ups!

K-State won the game!
Willie gave the players a high-five.

"Good job, Willie!"
the players shouted!

After the football game, Willie walked back to campus. It had been a long and fun day of Wildcat football.

Willie got home and climbed right into bed. Soon he was dreaming of another K-State victory. Goodnight, Willie.

Willie the Wildcat
and author, Dan Walter

**Join Willie the Wildcat
as he travels around the state of Kansas!
Available at local bookstores and online at
www.mascotbooks.com.**